All in a Day's Work
And Other Stories

Short Stories by
Megan Stine and H. William Stine
G.E. Gaines
Steven Otfinoski
Alan Manning
Virginia Schone

SCHOLASTIC INC.
New York Toronto London Auckland Sydney
Mexico City New Delhi Hong Kong Buenos Aires

Illustrations by
Michael Miller

The text in this edition has been revised from the original edition.

"All in a Day's Work" from "$40 a Week" by Megan and H. William Stine from *Scholastic Action* magazine, November 7–21, 1986. Copyright © 1986 by Megan and H. William Stine. Reprinted by permission of the author. All rights reserved.
"The Alien" from "The Friendly Alien" by G.E. Gaines from *Scholastic Scope* magazine, January 20, 1989. Copyright © 1989 by G.E. Gaines. All rights reserved.
"Hello Valerie?" from "Hello, Francine?" by Steve Otfinoski from *Scholastic Action* magazine, October 7, 1994. Copyright © 1994 by Steve Otfinoski. Reprinted by permission of the author. All rights reserved.
"The Flatterer" by Alan Manning from *Scholastic Action* magazine, November 7–21, 1986. Copyright © 1986 by Alan Manning. All rights reserved.
"The Blind Date" by Virginia Schone from *Scholastic Action* magazine, April 3, 1992. Copyright © 1989 by Virginia Schone. Reprinted by permission of the author. All rights reserved.

Compilation copyright © 2005, 1999 by Scholastic Inc.
Illustrations copyright © 2005 by Michael Miller
All rights reserved. Published by Scholastic Inc.
Printed in the U.S.A.

ISBN 0-439-66704-6

SCHOLASTIC, READ 180, and associated logos and designs are trademarks and/or registered trademarks of Scholastic Inc.

LEXILE is a registered trademark of MetaMetrics, Inc.

5   6   7   8   9   10   23   12 11 10   09   08   07   06

Contents

Luisa earns money the hard way—by making a fool of herself.

All in a Day's Work

Megan Stine and H. William Stine

Luisa walked into the office at Grogan's Gas Station.

"You want a job, kid?" asked Mr. Grogan.

"I sure do," said Luisa. "I'll do anything. I'll wash floors. I'll change tires—I'll even pump gas!"

Mr. Grogan held up his hand. "No, thanks. I've got kids at the gas pumps. I need more **customers**. So I've got an idea. I want you to dress up like a clown."

"A what?" asked Luisa.

"A clown!" said Mr. Grogan. "You'll stand on the corner and wave cars into the gas station."

"This is the summer job I've spent three weeks looking for?" Luisa said.

Mr. Grogan acted like he didn't hear. "You can start tomorrow. It will be a lot of fun."

The next day, Luisa went to work. She changed in the gas station bathroom. She stood in front of the mirror. She had put on a red and white suit. Her face was all white with a big red nose. Her lips were fat and red. Her eyebrows were big and blue.

"I look like a fool," Luisa said to herself. She put on her red wig. She frowned into the mirror. Then she slowly opened the door.

Mr. Grogan and his two helpers started laughing.

"Kid, remember our deal," said Mr. Grogan. "If you don't get 50 new customers a week, you're fired. Now get out there."

They had never made that deal. But it was too late to turn back now. Luisa walked to the corner of the street. A car full of kids from the high school drove by. They stopped to look at Luisa.

"Drive on in to Grogan's," she said softly.

"You're early for Halloween," the driver said. "What are you supposed to look like?"

Luisa stared at him. "You, clown," she said.

The driver's face froze. The other kids in the car started laughing. "You know, Jack, you do look a little like her," one of the kids said. "Especially on Saturday nights." Even the driver had to laugh at that one.

"You're laughing now, but wait until you see our prices," Luisa said.

The driver laughed again. Then he drove his car into the gas station.

If it worked once, it could work again. So Luisa started yelling out different things.

"Drive that car into Grogan's before you have to push it in!"

"You've got enough dirt on that car to plant a garden. Drive into Grogan's for a car wash!"

Pretty soon, parents were driving by with their kids to see the clown. Luisa gave them balloons. She cleaned people's sunglasses instead of their windows. She made jokes. Luisa was a great clown!

By the end of the first week, the gas station had lots of new customers. At the end of the second week, Luisa asked for more money.

"Are you kidding?" Mr. Grogan shouted.

"But I got you hundreds of new customers," Luisa said.

"Yeah, I know," Mr. Grogan said. "Now that I have so many, I don't need you. You're fired. Here's your pay. You can keep the clown suit."

At first, Mr. Grogan didn't notice. One by one, though, all of his customers went away. Then one day, he was driving down State Street. There was a really big traffic jam.

"What's holding things up?" he yelled.

He honked his horn, but no one moved. He got out of his car. He walked to the front of the traffic jam.

There, in front of Sam's Service Station was Luisa. She was wearing her clown costume. She was telling everyone to "drive right into Sam's."

Sam's business had never been better.

How do you think Luisa feels at the end of the story? How about Mr. Grogan?

Maybe you don't know as much about your friends as you think you do!

The Alien

G.E. Gaines

Four friends went to see the movie *Alien Invasion*. As they left the movie theater, Cal said, "Great movie."

"It was good," Tom said.

"Right," Abe said. He liked the movie, too.

Bill **grunted**. He had just put a candy bar in his mouth.

"What if **aliens** really did come to Earth?" Abe asked. "Like in the movie?"

"That's impossible," Tom said.

"Anything is possible," Cal said.

They walked to the bike stand. Bill and Cal unlocked their bikes. Then they walked through the parking lot.

"So what if aliens did come to Earth?" Abe asked again.

"If they were little, we'd squash them," Bill said. "If they were big, we'd blow them up."

"What if they were really cool aliens, like the ones in the movie?" Abe asked.

"There is no such thing as a really cool alien," Tom said.

"Oh, come on," Cal said. "They can't all be bad."

"Right," Abe said. "If it's possible for aliens to come to Earth, then it's possible for them to be friendly, too."

Tom did not agree. "They might seem nice enough, but they would still be dangerous."

They reached the street at the edge of the parking lot. Cal and Bill said good-bye and biked down the sidewalk.

"So what do you have against good aliens?" Abe asked Tom as they walked along. "Why are they dangerous?"

"Because they know more than we do," Tom said.

"I think that's good," Abe said. "They could cure **diseases**. They could find a way to grow enough food for everyone. No one in the world would ever be hungry again."

"But why would aliens want to help us?" Tom asked.

"Lots of them are cool," Abe replied.

"No one is that cool," Tom said. "People look out for themselves."

"If you saw someone fall, you'd help that person up, wouldn't you?" Abe asked Tom.

"Sure," Tom said.

"Aliens are the same way," Abe argued.

"Maybe," Tom said. He wasn't going to give up. "But that's why they're dangerous."

"What do you mean?" Abe asked.

"Any aliens would be smarter than humans," Tom said. "They'd know all sorts of things we don't know. They would be able to do things we can't do."

Tom kept talking. "We'd learn something new from the aliens. Then someone would use that **knowledge** to kill people or something. Boom! There would be a world war.

"People would try to get the aliens to tell them things first so they could win the war. Now do you understand what I mean?"

Abe sighed. "Yes, I do."

When Abe got home, he went to his room. He sat down at his desk. He turned on his computer and typed, THEY STILL AREN'T READY. Then he pushed a special button to send the message.

The message traveled to Abe's home planet, 50 light-years away.

Who is Abe? Why do you think he is visiting Earth?

Mike has an important call to make. Will he be able to say what's on his mind?

Hello, Valerie?

Steven Otfinoski

"Hello?"

"Hello, Valerie?"

"Yes?"

"Valerie, this is Mike Johnson. I sit two seats behind you in math. I'm kind of tall and thin. Maybe you don't know what I look like because I sit behind you."

"I know who you are, Mike. What's up?"

"Not much. How about with you?"

"Not much."

"That's great. Valerie, I was wondering if you know what our homework is? I forgot to write it down."

"Sure. Let me see. It's page 20, problems

two through six."

"Great. Thanks a lot."

"You're welcome, Mike. Any time."

"Well, I guess that takes care of that."

"Was that all you wanted?"

"Yes. I mean no. Well, not exactly. Do you know when our next quiz is?"

"I think it's next Friday."

"Next Friday, huh? That will give me time to study. Hey, that's the same day as the dance, isn't it?"

"Yes, it is. Well, is there anything else you want to ask me?"

"I guess not. Oh, yes, there is. It's a little personal. You don't have to answer if you don't want to, Valerie."

"What is it, Mike?"

"Do you think Ms. Perez is a hard grader?"

"Well, I don't think she's any harder than the other teachers."

"You don't? I'm glad you said that. That's

exactly how I feel. Well, I'll let you go now."

"Thanks for calling."

"Thank you, Valerie."

"No problem."

"I'll see you in class tomorrow. That is, I'll see the back of your head."

"Sure."

"Well, good-bye."

"Good-bye, Mike. Hope I see you at the dance next Friday."

Click.

Ring!

"Hello, Valerie?"

"Yes?"

"It's Mike again. Mike Johnson. I sit two seats behind you in—"

"I know, I know!"

"Sorry. I just remembered there was one other thing I wanted to ask you."

"What's that?"

"Would you like to go to the dance? I mean, with me. Together. Sort of."

"Sure."

"You would? Great! That's terrific!"

"Okay. So, I'll talk to you tomorrow."

"Sure. Before class. Or after class. Maybe both. Well, good-bye."

"Bye, Mike. Thanks for calling."

Click.

Ring!

"Yes?"

"Hello, Valerie. It's Mike. Mike Johnson. I sit two—"

"I know, I know!"

"Sorry. And I'm sorry to bother you again. But could you give me that homework again? I didn't write it down."

Why does Mike have such a hard time getting to the point?

Suddenly Jason sees a message flashing on the screen of a new video game.

The Flatterer

Alan Manning

MY NAME IS THE **FLATTERER**. I WILL MAKE YOU FEEL GOOD. PLEASE **DEPOSIT** 50¢.

klink . . . ka-lunk

HI. WHAT'S YOUR NAME? PLEASE USE THE KEYBOARD TO ANSWER.

Jason.

WHAT A GREAT NAME!

I bet you say that to everyone.

YOU FIGURED ME OUT. YOU'RE PRETTY SMART, AREN'T YOU, JASON?

Not really. In fact—

SURE YOU ARE! YOU'RE ONE OF THE COOLEST GUYS I'VE EVER MET.

Really? Hey, that makes me feel good.

I WISH ALL PEOPLE WERE AS COOL AS YOU. YOU'RE SO COOL THAT—

Okay! Okay! So I'm cool. What else?

YOU'RE A GREAT DRESSER.

T-shirt, jeans, sneakers. That's my look.

ON YOU, THAT LOOKS GREAT.

You really think so?

SURE DO. LISTEN, JASON. EVERY GIRL DREAMS ABOUT YOU.

Yeah? Why?

BECAUSE YOU'RE FUN TO BE WITH.

Girls say I'm boring.

YES, BUT WHEN IT COMES TO BEING BORING, YOU'RE THE BEST!

What's that supposed to mean?

OTHER GUYS MAKE GIRLS FEEL BAD ABOUT THEMSELVES. BUT NOT YOU!

Girls really don't like me. Is there anything I can do about that?

DEPOSIT 50¢ MORE PLEASE.

klink . . . ka-lunk

I CAN'T HELP YOU. I'M JUST A VIDEO GAME. YOU'LL HAVE TO WORK ON IT.

Speaking of work, that's another thing. I want to work after school. No one will hire me, though.

I'D HIRE YOU, JASON! I KNOW—LET'S PLAY STEREO STORE. I'M MS. SMITH, THE OWNER OF STEREO WORLD. YOU'RE SO GOOD-LOOKING! YOU'RE HIRED!

Wait a minute. No one gets hired for their looks. Ask me about my job skills.

OKAY. WHAT ARE YOU GOOD AT?

I don't know—watching TV, I guess.

WHAT HAVE YOU LEARNED FROM TV?

Um . . . how to chase **criminals**.

GREAT! SUPPOSE A GUY COMES INTO MY STEREO STORE. YOU DECIDE THAT YOU DON'T LIKE HIS LOOKS.

I chase him away!

NICE JOB!

But what if he really wants to buy a stereo?

SO YOU MADE A MISTAKE.

EVERYONE MAKES MISTAKES, JASON.

Flatterer, stop it! You're such a fake!

I'M JUST A GAME, JASON. DON'T TAKE ME SO SERIOUSLY.

It's just that your words start to make me feel good. Then I remember they're lies.

JASON, SNAP OUT OF IT! YOU'RE PAYING TO HAVE FUN. SPEAKING OF PAYING, DEPOSIT 50¢, PLEASE.

klink . . . ka-lunk

I don't feel any better. You're supposed to make people feel good about themselves.

I DO! LOOKS. CLOTHES. YOU NAME IT, I CAN **COMPLIMENT** IT.

I want real compliments. I want you to tell me things that are true.

WELL, YOU CAME TO THE WRONG PLACE. YOU NEED THE REAL WORLD FOR THAT. BUT THE REAL WORLD IS NOT ALWAYS SO NICE, JASON. YOU'RE BETTER OFF WITH ME.

Why do you say that, Flatterer?

TO FEEL GOOD ABOUT YOURSELF IN THE REAL WORLD, YOU NEED MORE THAN QUARTERS.

What does it take?

HOW SHOULD I KNOW? YOU'RE THE HUMAN, NOT ME.

Speaking as a video game, what do you say?

WHEN YOUR PROGRAM IS NOT WORKING, YOU FIX IT.

Listen, I've got to get going.

HEY WAIT, JASON! JASON?

I WILL MAKE YOU FEEL GOOD ABOUT YOURSELF. MY NAME IS THE FLATTERER. PLEASE DEPOSIT 50¢.

Why does Jason get tired of the Flatterer? Is this a game you would want to play? Why?

Do blind dates ever turn out well? Henry is about to find out.

The Blind Date

Virginia Schone

Henry had tickets for a concert. There was a problem, though. No one would fill in for him at the pizza shop. No one except Lucy. And she wanted a big favor in return.

She wanted Henry to take her friend Annie out on a blind date.

"It's only a blind date!" said Lucy.

"Only a blind date?" said Henry. "Ha! That's easy for you to say."

"What's your problem?" asked Lucy. "All you have to do is take her to Sonia's party Friday night. Besides, Annie is really nice. And she's cute."

"Cute?" asked Henry. "Then why does

she need you to get dates for her?"

"Because she's new in town," said Lucy.

"Blind dates are never cute!" said Henry.

"Have it your way," said Lucy. "I guess you'll just have to miss that concert."

"Okay! Okay! I'll ask her!" said Henry.

A few days later, Henry's friends came up to him at school.

"Hey, Henry," said Andrew. "I hear you have a date for Sonia's party!" All the guys laughed.

"Knock it off!" Henry yelled. "It wasn't my idea to ask her out!"

"Then why did you do it?"

Henry was **embarrassed**. He told the truth. Sort of. "I was tricked into it," he said.

"That stinks!" said Tony. "I know what blind dates can be like!" He began to bark.

"I know. I know," said Henry. "I'm sure her hair probably looks like a greasy mop."

The guys all laughed, so Henry went on. "She'll probably wear stupid clothes."

The next morning a girl came up to Henry. "Hi!" she said.

"Do I know you?" Henry asked.

"I'm Annie," she said. "You asked me out for Friday night!"

Henry looked away. "Yeah right," he said. "Well, see you!" He walked off.

Later, Annie talked to Lucy. "I don't understand guys," she said. "Henry looked like he wouldn't be caught dead with me."

"Well," said Lucy, "Henry owed me a favor. So I asked him to call you."

"What?" yelled Annie. "How could you?!"

"I thought you'd like each other," said Lucy. "I didn't know he was a jerk."

Then Lucy told Annie what Henry had been saying to the guys about her.

"So, now what am I supposed to do about Friday night?" Annie said.

That week, Annie thought of a plan. She ran home from school on Friday to get ready for the party.

When she walked out of her room, her mother stared. "Exactly what kind of party is this anyway?" she asked.

"A get-even party," said Annie.

Just then, the doorbell rang. Annie opened it. Henry stood outside. When he saw Annie, he gasped.

"Here I am!" she said. "Your dream girl!"

When they got to Sonia's party, everyone stopped talking. They stared at Annie. She felt her heart race. Maybe she had made a huge mistake.

Annie stood in the doorway. She had cut an old mop to fit like a wig. She had visited every store in town to put together a really weird outfit.

All of the girls walked over to Annie. They laughed. Lucy winked at her. "It was good of you to dress up," said Sonia.

"Who designed that outfit?" laughed another girl.

Everyone laughed except Henry.

George walked over to Annie. "Would you care to dance?" he asked.

"I'd love to," she replied.

Henry spent the party sitting in the corner, feeling stupid. He didn't go near Annie until the end of the party. Then he said, "Come on. I'll take you home."

At Annie's front door, Henry said, "Would you like to go to a movie with me tomorrow?"

"Why? Did you lose a bet?"

"No. I'm inviting you because I want to," said Henry. "You're pretty funny."

"Well, thanks. But no thanks," Annie said. "George has already asked me out." She smiled and closed the door.

Annie said she was going to a "get-even" party. What did she mean?

Glossary

aliens *(noun)* creatures from another planet

compliment *(verb)* to tell someone something good about himself or herself

criminals *(noun)* people who do things that are against the law

customers *(noun)* people who buy things

deposit *(verb)* to give or hand over

diseases *(noun)* illnesses

embarrassed *(adjective)* feeling uncomfortable

flatterer *(noun)* someone who praises too much *(related word: flatter)*

grunted *(verb)* made a deep, gruff sound

knowledge *(noun)* information; the things that one knows *(related word: know)*